DAY AND NIGHT

Heather Amery
Illustrated by Peter Firmin
Text revised by Karen Bryant-Mole

Consultant Betty Root
Centre for the Teaching of Reading
University of Reading, England

Morning on the farm

The hens and the pigs are having their breakfast.
Which pig do you think is the mummy pig?
The cows have been milked and are going to the fields.
What noises do you think all the animals are making?

Evening on the farm

The animals are going to bed. The cows are coming back from the fields to spend the night in the barn.

Can you find a bird sitting on the fence? Do you know what it is?

Find the boy wearing blue trousers. What is he doing?

Morning in the street

Everyone is very busy. Can you spot a newspaper delivery boy and a window cleaner? What jobs do you think the other people do? A shopkeeper is putting a price label on the grapefruit. What other sorts of fruit can you see?

Evening in the street

The people are going home from work. Can you find someone reading a newspaper and someone eating a banana? The shops are closing for the night. The shopkeepers have to tidy up their shop and put away all the boxes. How many boxes is the man carrying?

Morning in the bedroom

It is time for the children to get up. Can you find someone who has washed his face and is drying himself with a towel? What is the other boy doing? The girl is opening the curtains. Can you see the bird singing on the branch outside her window?

It is time for the children to go to bed. The stars are shining in the dark sky. Someone is already asleep. Who is it? Can you see that all the toys have been tidied away? Look at the girl's bed. What do you think she will have to do before she goes to sleep?

Morning in the kitchen

Everyone is having breakfast. Mummy is eating a piece of toast. What is daddy going to eat? Someone has spilled the milk. Who is enjoying a surprise drink? There are four children in the family. Which one do you think is the youngest?

Evening in the kitchen

Most of the family are having their supper. Someone has already gone to bed. Who is it? Can you find the dog? He is begging for some food. The cat is having another drink of milk. What is she drinking it from this time?

Morning in the house

It is time to go to school. Everyone looks neat and tidy. Who is helping the girl do up her coat buttons? One of the children doesn't go to school yet. Which one do you think it is?

Evening in the house

The children are home from school. They look as though they have had a tiring day.
The dog is pleased to see the children home again. He wants to play with them.
The cat is already playing with someone. Who is she playing with?

Morning at the campsite

There is lots of work to be done before breakfast.
Can you see someone filling up a bucket with water?
One man has already filled two special water carriers. Can you find him?
Someone else is cooking on a little camping cooker. Can you find him too?

Evening at the campsite

The grown-ups are having a barbecue supper.
Most of the children are asleep in their tents. How many are still awake?
There are seven different types of animal in this picture.
See if you can spot them all.

Daytime in the hospital

The children have already had breakfast. The nurse is taking one boy's pulse.
He has a thermometer in his mouth. Do you know what a thermometer measures?
What are all the children doing? What can you see driving past the window?

Night-time in the hospital

It is very quiet now.
Only one child is awake. Can you find her?
One of the children has broken his leg. He has a plaster cast to keep the bones in the right place.
Can you see the wheels on the beds?
These make it easier for the nurses to move the beds around.

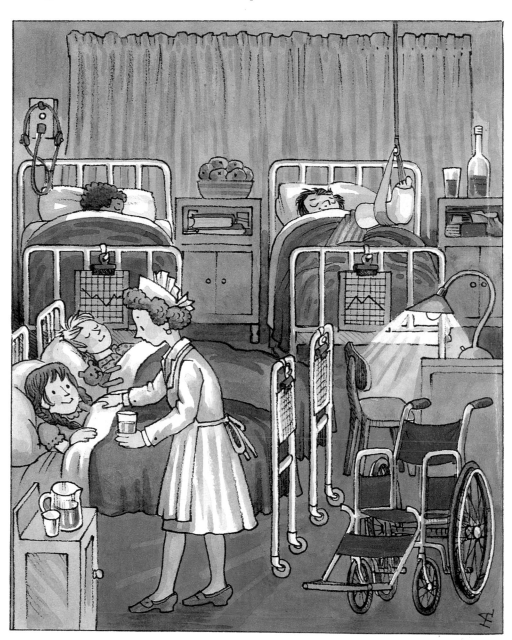

Daytime in the harbour

The fishing boats have just come in. The fishermen are using a hoist to unload a net full of fish.
Can you see two seagulls who both want the same fish? Can you find two more seagulls? There is a big lobster in a lobster pot. Whose nose is he trying to pinch?

Night-time in the harbour

The fishermen are setting off for the night's work.

If you look very carefully at the nearest boat you can see a red light on one side and a green light on the other.

Can you see something that will guide the fishermen back to the harbour when they have finished their work?

Day in the café

It is lunchtime in the café. The customers are hungry, so the waiter and waitress are very busy. How many plates is the waitress carrying? The café has a highchair for its very young customers. What is the girl in the highchair wearing to protect her dress?

Night in the café

The café is closed to customers but there is still a lot of work to be done. What are the waiter and waitresses doing now?

Look around the café and see if you can find some other jobs that need to be done before they can go home?

Day in the pet shop

There are lots of animals in the pet shop. Do you know what they all are?
The door of the bird cage is open. Who do you think usually lives there?
One of the boys is going to buy a pet. Which animal do you think he might buy?

Night in the pet shop

Many of the animals are asleep but some are still awake. Which ones are still awake? Can you see the basket and some leads hanging on the wall? There are also some kennels on the floor. What pet might you have if you needed these things?

Day in the street

A car has stopped at the pedestrian crossing to let some people cross the road. Who else is crossing the road?

See if you can find a traffic warden and two men digging a hole.

A man is watering his window boxes. What colour are the flowers?

Night in the street

Most people have gone home but some people work at night.

Where do you think the firemen are going?

The big hole that the men dug has lights all around it.

Why do you think the lights are there?

Puzzle picture

Would you see these things in the morning, during the day or at night?

First published in 1985 by Usborne Publishing Ltd, Usborne House, 83-85 Saffron Hill, London, EC1N 8RT, England. Revised edition published 1990. Copyright © 1990, 1985 Usborne Publishing Ltd. All rights reserved. No part of this publication may be reproduced, stored in a retrieval system, or transmitted by any means, electronic, mechanical, photocopying, recording or otherwise, without the prior permission of the publisher. The name Usborne and the device 🎈 are the Trade Marks of Usborne Publishing Ltd.

Printed in Belgium